To my amazing sister, Nancy Kiefer.
Without her knowledge, encouragement,
and dedication, the Lindie Lou
Adventure Series would not exist.

Lindie Lou®
brings joy,
gives comfort,
cares,
feels,
pleases,
loves,
and
inspires.
Need I ask for more?

—Jeanne Bender

Here's what kids told Jeanne Bender about Lindie Lou!

Thank you for video calling our class! I love Lindie Lou! I've learned lots of new things. I like searching for hints to where she will go in the next book. -Maria

The sliding game is so funny! Jasper is my favorite puppy. –Evan

I'd like to read more about Lindie Lou's brothers and sisters in some of the other books. I really like Diamond. –Rebecca

I like the song on your website lindielou.com. I can't get it out of my head! La la la, la la la la la, la la la la, la la la. -Emma

I like the color pictures. Lindie Lou is so cute. -Elizabeth

I like the short chapters and the way they end. I always want to know what will happen next! I can't wait to read the next book. -Jonathan

Contents

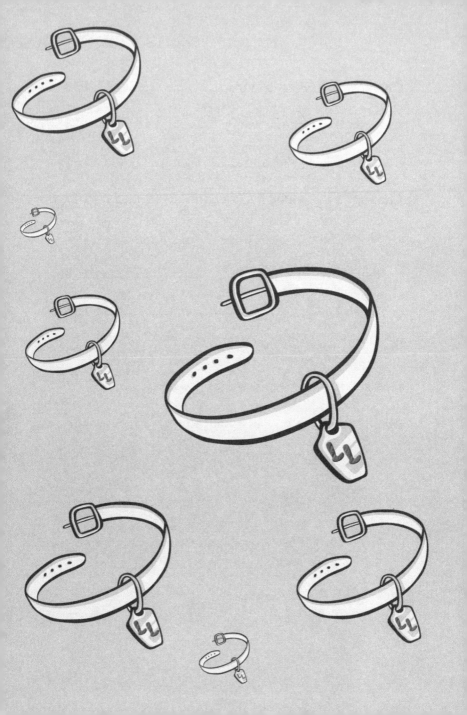

Lindie Lou®

Adventure Series

Flying High

Flying on an Airplane for the Very First Time!

by Jeanne Bender
illustrated by Kate Willows

PINA PUBLISHING ❂ SEATTLE

PINA PUBLISHING ♦ SEATTLE

Text copyright © 2016, 2018 by Jeanne Bender
Illustrations by Kate Willows © 2016, 2018 for J.A. Zehrer Group, LLC
Cover and book design by Susan Harring © 2018 for J.A. Zehrer Group, LLC

Lindie Lou is a registered trademark of J.A. Zehrer Group, LLC.

For information about special discounts for bulk purchases, go to:
lindielou.com/contact-us.html
Manufactured in the United States of America
Library of Congress Cataloging-in-Publication Data Bender, Jeanne

Summary: Lindie Lou is an adorable puppy who loves an adventure. She is named after her father, Lynwood Lou Peek-a-boo because they both have huge front paws. But, Lindie Lou looks just like her mother, Molly. They both have soft brown fur, long floppy ears, and big green eyes. Her owners, Joe and Sherry promised the puppy who looks the most like Molly to a family member who lives in the Emerald City.

"I want to keep Lindie Lou," said Joe.

"A promise is a promise," replied Sherry.

Lindie Lou's adventures take her outside for the first time, to a museum with a ten-story slide, on a *puppy play date* with children from a local shelter, and on an airplane for the very first time.

Come along for the ride while Lindie Lou learns life lessons, discovers what it's like to find a best friend, flies above the clouds with a wise dog named Max, and arrives in the Emerald City.

"I can promise you this Lindie Lou," said Max. "Your life has only just begun little one."

ISBN: 978-1-943493-24-1 (hardcover)
ISBN: 978-1-943493-22-7 (softcover)
ISBN: 978-1-943493-23-4 (e-book)

[1. Adventure Stories. 2. Pets–Fiction. 3. Dogs–Fiction. 4. Airplanes Fiction.
5. Fall Fiction. 6. Travel Fiction. 7. Pet Adoption Fiction. 8. Juvenile Fiction.]

Chapter 1

THE PUPPY PLAYGROUND

On a warm August day, Molly pushed the kitchen door open. Her five furry puppies ran to greet her.

She dropped to the floor and rolled on her side. One of the puppies played with Molly's fluffy tail. His name was Topaz. He was a golden color and was very frisky. Another puppy climbed up Molly's leg. Her name was Diamond. She had shiny black fur and seemed very shy. A reddish-brown puppy named Ruby, was sitting near Molly's tummy. She was the smallest of the puppies. Jasper looked over at Ruby. He was

black-and-white. He bent down and wiggled his tail. Jasper was about to jump on Ruby when Lindie Lou ran into him. They rolled on the floor, sat up, and shook their heads.

Lindie Lou reached over and grabbed one of Molly's long floppy ears. Molly swung her head from side to side.

Lindie Lou hung on with her huge front paws. She enjoyed the ride.

"They are so cute,**"** said Sherry. She was sitting at the kitchen table.
"I just love to watch them play."

"So do I," said Joe. He was standing by the window. "Sherry, I've been thinking. The puppies are growing so fast. We're going to have to find a larger place for them to live. The kitchen is getting too small."

"Maybe we can fix up the garage," said Sherry.

Joe looked out the window. The garage was next to the house. He didn't use it much. He liked to park his truck outside.

Joe and Sherry lived in an orange brick house on the edge of a big green park. On the other side of the park was the city of Saint Louis.

"The garage would be a great place for the puppies," said Joe.

"Let's make it real nice and call it the Puppy Playground," said Sherry.

"Great idea," replied Joe.

Sherry turned and looked at Molly. She was still playing with her puppies.

"Which one should we keep?" asked Sherry.

"I like Lindie Lou, because she looks like her mom," said Joe.

Lindie Lou was sitting on the floor near Molly. She did look a lot like her Mom. They both had soft brown fur, long floppy ears,

and big green eyes. But Lindie Lou was named after her dad, Lynwood Lou Peek-a-Boo, because they both had **huge** paws.

Sherry looked over at the puppies.

"They are all so cute," said Sherry.

Joe nodded.

The next day Joe cleaned out the garage. He painted the walls a bright white color and the floor a soft tan.

Joe installed a large window so Molly and her puppies would have more light. Then, he put in a doggy door.

The Puppy Playground needed a bed, so Sherry went shopping. She found a large black one with gray-and-white stripes.

Then Sherry picked out some stuffed animals for the puppies to play with.

The last thing she found was a pile of soft blankets. They had paw prints on them. Sherry picked up five blankets. One for each of the puppies.

Sherry put the bed in the middle of the room. She filled a box with the stuffed animals and pushed it into the corner. Then she tossed the blankets on the floor.

"This place looks great," said Sherry. "It is now ready for the puppies."

Sherry walked back into the kitchen. She watched the puppies play for a few minutes. She picked up the puppies two at a time. Then she carried them into the Puppy Playground and set them on the floor. She brought Lindie Lou in last. Lindie Lou reached up and licked Sherry on the nose.

"You are so sweet," said Sherry. She lifted up one of Lindie Lou's paws. "Look at your huge paws." Sherry rolled Lindie Lou over and tickled her tummy. Lindie Lou smiled and wiggled her legs. Sherry giggled. Then she set Lindie Lou on the floor. Lindie Lou ran over to one of the blankets. She sniffed it, plopped down, stuck out her tongue, and sighed.

Ruby turned around. She saw the ramp leading up to the doggy bed. She climbed up the ramp and sat down. Ruby was very proud because she was the first puppy to sit on their new bed.

Jasper bounced up the ramp and sat next to Ruby. He pushed her to one side and rolled onto his back.

Diamond climbed up on a wooden chair. She was now taller than all the other puppies.

Topaz looked for something to play with. He tipped his head and looked over at the box of stuffed animals.

The Puppy Playground was a great idea, thought Sherry. *I think I'll give the puppies some time to enjoy their new home.*

Sherry smiled and quietly left the room.

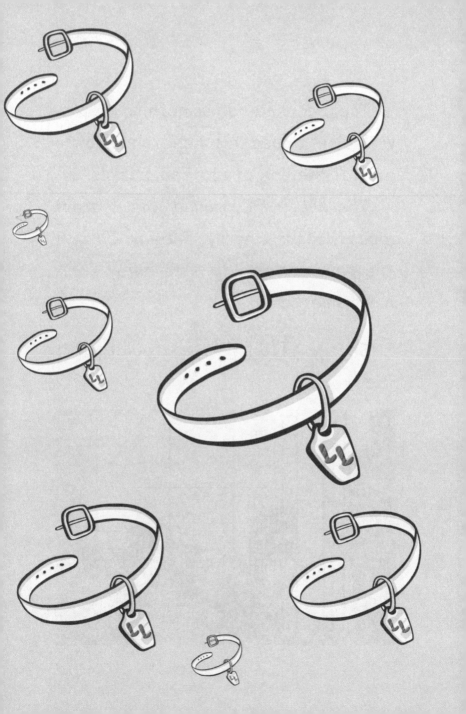

Chapter 2

THE SLIDING GAME

Later that day, Molly pushed the doggy door open. All of the puppies ran to greet her. She walked over to the window and lay down. This time Lindie Lou climbed on top of her mom's back. She sat up and looked around the room.

Lindie Lou saw Topaz

around on the floor. He was on one of

the blankets. She wanted to play on a blanket too. So, Lindie Lou slid off of Molly's back and ran to one of the empty blankets. She jumped on the blanket and her huge paws slipped away. Lindie Lou plopped down on her stomach.

Topaz   Jasper

She looked like a pancake. Sherry was watching from the doorway. She laughed at Lindie Lou.

Lindie Lou looked up at Jasper. He was getting ready to play a game.

Lindie Lou   Ruby   Diamond

Sherry called it the *sliding game.*

Jasper walked over to one end of the room. All the other puppies followed, except for Lindie Lou. She decided to watch her brothers and sisters play.

Jasper started to run. When he reached the middle of the room, he rolled on his back, and slid across the floor.

He slid so fast, he **crashed** into the wall. The other puppies followed. They also slid across the floor. When they reached the other side, they all ran into Jasper.

Lindie Lou jumped up. She ran to one end of the room. Then she turned around near the box of stuffed animals. Jasper and Topaz were right behind her. Ruby came next. Diamond followed Ruby.

Lindie Lou ran to the middle of the room. Instead of sliding on her back, she slid on her belly. She stuck out her huge front paws. They were so big and furry they helped her slide faster than the other puppies. Lindie Lou hit the wall first and the puppies slid into her.

"You all look like fuzzy little round balls," said Sherry.

She laughed out loud.

Lindie Lou rolled on her back. Sherry walked over and tickled her tummy. She was singing a song.

YOU ARE MY

LITTLE LINDIE LOU

AND I LOVE YOU

La La La

La La La La La

La La La

La La

I want to keep Lindie Lou, thought Sherry. But her sister Kate asked for a puppy who looked just like Molly. Lindie Lou was the ONLY puppy who looked like Molly. This sweet puppy was going to live with Kate and her husband Bryan, in the Emerald City, as soon as she was old enough to travel. There was nothing Sherry could do about it.

A promise is a promise.

Joe said it was up to Sherry to pick one of the puppies to live with them. She looked around the room. All the puppies were together. They were playing and climbing all over each other.

They are all so sweet, thought Sherry. It made her want to sing.

La La La

La La La La La

La La La

La La

I like the song Sherry is singing, thought Lindie Lou. She swayed to the music. All of the other puppies joined Lindie Lou.

The puppies were happy in the Puppy Playground and wanted to live there for the rest of their lives.

Lindie Lou Song

Chorus 1
LA LA LA
LA LA LA LA LA
LA LA LA LA
LA LA LA

Chorus 2
LA LA LA
LA LA LA LA LA
LA LA LA
LA LA

Verse 1
L-I-N-D-I-E
L-O-U spells
Lindie Lou

Verse 4
I can't wait
To see
Where you
Take me

Chorus 2
LA LA LA
LA LA LA LA LA
LA LA LA
LA LA

Chorus 2
LA LA LA
LA LA LA LA LA
LA LA LA
LA LA

Verse 2
Lindie Lou
You are cool
And your friends think
You're a jewel

(Pause)

Chorus 1
LA LA LA
LA LA LA LA LA
LA LA LA LA
LA LA LA

Chorus 2
LA LA LA
LA LA LA LA LA
LA LA LA
LA LA

Verse 5
You are my
Little Lindie Lou
And I love you

Verse 3
You are a
Very lucky girl
'Cuz you've been
All over the world

Chorus 2
LA LA LA
LA LA LA LA LA
LA LA LA
LA LA

Go to lindielou.com **to listen to the Lindie Lou Song.**

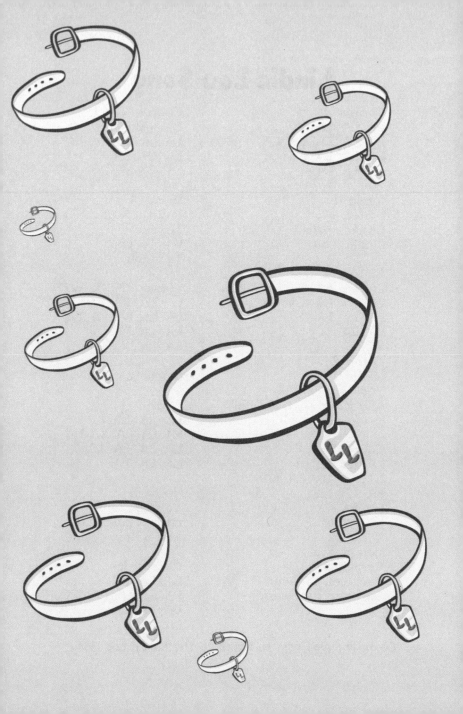

Chapter 3

LINDIE LOU MEETS COCO

Lindie Lou woke up from a long nap. Her brothers and sisters were playing on the doggy bed. She watched Diamond hold Ruby down. Ruby turned over onto her back. All four of her legs were kicking in the air.

Topaz pushed Jasper off the doggy bed. He landed on his head. Jasper sat up. He was so **dizzy,** his head rolled around and around. All the other puppies laughed at the funny face he made.

Lindie Lou felt stiff after her long nap. She slowly stood up and stretched out her huge front paws. This made Lindie Lou's tail lift up and her tongue stick out. She wiggled her tail and looked at Sherry.

Sherry was sitting on the wooden chair. She laughed at Lindie Lou.

Lindie Lou smiled. Her tongue was still sticking out. Sherry started to sing.

LINDIE LOU
YOU ARE COOL
AND YOUR FRIENDS THINK
YOU'RE A JEWEL
La La La
La La La La La
La La La
La La

Lindie Lou liked when Sherry sang. She had a sweet voice.

Lindie Lou stood up and looked around the room. She walked over to the box of stuffed animals. *Maybe I can find a special toy,* she thought. Lindie Lou put one of her huge paws on the box

and then the other. Then she jumped inside.

A fuzzy white rabbit and a gray mouse were on top of the pile. Lindie Lou pushed them aside. Under the rabbit was a black cat. Lindie Lou sniffed it and kept digging. She saw two little black eyes looking up at her. It was a monkey, and he was smiling.

Lindie Lou grabbed the monkey in her mouth. She turned and looked around the Puppy Playground. *I must find a safe place to hide you,* she thought.

Lindie Lou jumped out of the box and walked over to her favorite blanket.

I better not hide him under here, thought Lindie Lou. *He would be too easy to see because there would be a*

 *in the blanket.*

Maybe I can hide him under the doggy bed, thought Lindie Lou. She walked over, bent down, and tried to push him under the bed. But he didn't fit.

Lindie Lou looked around the room. She didn't see any good places to hide her new friend. She started digging at the floor. *I can't even dig a hole to hide him in,* she thought.

Lindie Lou started to panic. She ran back and forth in a

pattern until she ended up on the other side of the Puppy Playground. Sherry was sitting on a chair. She was reading a book. Sherry didn't see Lindie Lou push the monkey under the chair.

This is a great spot, thought Lindie Lou. She looked around the room. They were far away from all of the action and Sherry was near. She made Lindie Lou feel safe.

"I will call you... **Coco**," whispered Lindie Lou. She leaned under the chair and licked the monkey's face. Then she sat down near Sherry's feet.

Sherry bent down and scratched Lindie Lou on the head. Lindie Lou put her paw on Sherry's foot.

With Coco safely tucked away, Lindie Lou decided to go and play with her brothers and sisters. She saw Topaz climb into the box of stuffed animals. He grabbed the gray mouse and jumped out of the box. Then he dropped the mouse on the floor. Topaz held it down with one of his paws and tore a hole in it. Then he pulled its stuffing out.

Lindie Lou couldn't believe what she was **seeing**.

Topaz was turning into quite the troublemaker. Lindie Lou opened her mouth and let out a WOOf!!!

I'm glad I found Coco before Topaz did, thought Lindie Lou. *Otherwise, he might look like that gray mouse!*

Lindie Lou turned around and looked at Coco. He was still lying safely under the chair. Sherry was still reading her book. Lindie Lou sighed and turned back toward her brothers and sisters.

*I learned an **important lesson** today,* thought Lindie Lou.

If you have something you care about, put it in a safe place.

Bang went the doggy door.

Molly walked in with a giant treat in her mouth. The puppies tried to grab it from her, but Molly lifted her head high enough that the treat was out of reach.

Jasper climbed up on the doggy bed. He leaped off its edge and grabbed the treat in his mouth. His paws hit the floor and the treat came crashing down.

Jasper dragged the treat over to one of the blankets. The other puppies ran after him. The treat was big enough for all of them to share.

Joe must be home, thought Sherry. *He must have given Molly the treat.* Sherry stood up and left the Puppy Playground.

After finishing her part of the treat, Lindie Lou went to check on **Coco**. He was still under the chair. She pulled him close and put her chin on his head.

Lindie Lou found a new friend that day and wanted to keep him safe, forever.

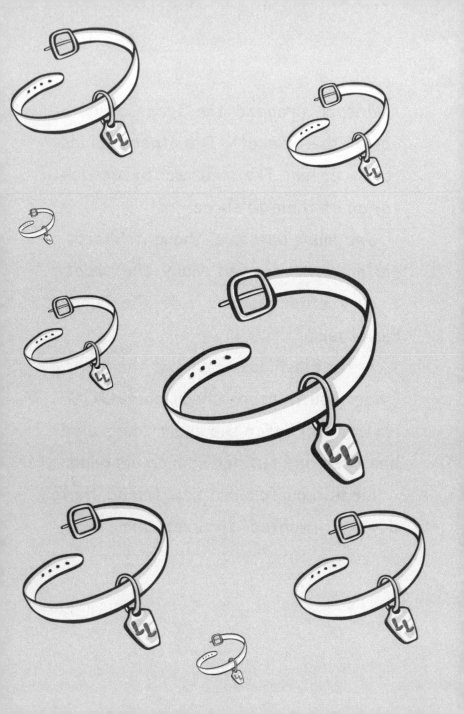

Chapter 4

OUTSIDE

The autumn sun streamed through the window in the Puppy Playground. It reached across the floor. The light woke up Lindie Lou. She was taking a nap. She moved her head away from the light and slowly opened her eyes. After a while, Lindie Lou stretched out her huge front paws. She yawned, rolled over, and slowly stood up. Lindie Lou followed the light beam on the floor. It led her to the other side of the Puppy Playground. She was about to look out the window when she heard a loud rumbling noise. It was so

LOUD

it made her shake. She turned around and ran away. Coco was underneath the wooden chair. Lindie Lou ran to him. She picked him up and held him in her mouth.

The noise scared the other puppies too. They all ran and hid behind the doggy bed.

Suddenly, the noise stopped and the room was quiet again.

The puppies looked at one another. They didn't know what was happening. They listened for a moment. They heard footsteps coming toward the door. The puppies started barking. Lindie Lou didn't make a sound. She still had Coco in her mouth. The door swung open and Joe walked in.

"Oh, did I scare you?" he asked. He noticed that they were hiding from him. "Come over here puppies. It's me, Joe. You know who I am. Let's have some playtime."

Joe knelt down on the floor. The puppies ran to him. He tickled their tummies and scratched their backs. Lindie Lou set Coco down and ran to Joe. He lifted her up and gave her a soft hug.

Joe loved the puppies and knew he would miss them. Today they turned eight weeks old. They were now old enough to travel and it was time for some of them to leave.

Joe saw Topaz sitting near the doggy bed. He put Lindie Lou down, reached over, and picked him up. Then he scooped up Ruby.

Ruby looked at Lindie Lou. Somehow, she knew she was leaving. Lindie Lou looked up at Ruby as if it was for the last time. Then Joe turned toward the door.

"It's getting late," called Sherry from inside the house. "You don't want the puppies to miss their airplanes."

What's an airplane? thought Lindie Lou.

Topaz was going to live with Sherry's cousin, Ronda. She owned a farm and had lots of animals to play with. Ruby was going to live with Joe's sister, Linda. She had two daughters and lived on an island.

"I'm on it," Joe replied.

With Topaz and Ruby under his arm, Joe rushed out of the Puppy Playground. He left in such a hurry, he forgot to shut the door.

The loud noise started again.

Lindie Lou ran to see what it was. She looked out the open door. The rumbling was coming from a big blue truck. Joe, Topaz, and Ruby were driving away in it.

Lindie Lou was confused. *Should I go after them? Where are they going? Can I go outside?*

Lindie Lou looked back at Jasper and Diamond. They were hiding behind the doggy bed. *Maybe I shouldn't go outside,* thought Lindie Lou.

For some reason Lindie Lou wasn't afraid. She turned to the open door and ran outside.

Lindie Lou ran down the driveway after the truck. It was moving very fast. The truck left behind a big cloud of dust. Lindie Lou turned around to avoid the dust, but it covered her up.

She waited for the air to clear. When it did, Lindie Lou saw things she had never seen before.

She saw giant trees with red, orange, and yellow leaves. The ground around the trees was covered with leaves. They were more colorful than anything Lindie Lou had ever seen. She wanted to roll around in them.

Lindie Lou ran to a pile of leaves and jumped in. She sat up and shook

her head. The leaves went flying everywhere.

Lindie Lou sniffed the leaves. They made her sneeze. The leaves smelled fresh on top and musty underneath. Lindie Lou disappeared in the pile of leaves. She liked rolling around in the bright, crunchy colors. When she jumped out, some of the leaves stuck to her fur. Lindie Lou shook as hard as she could, but the leaves stayed put.

I think I look like a tree, giggled Lindie Lou.

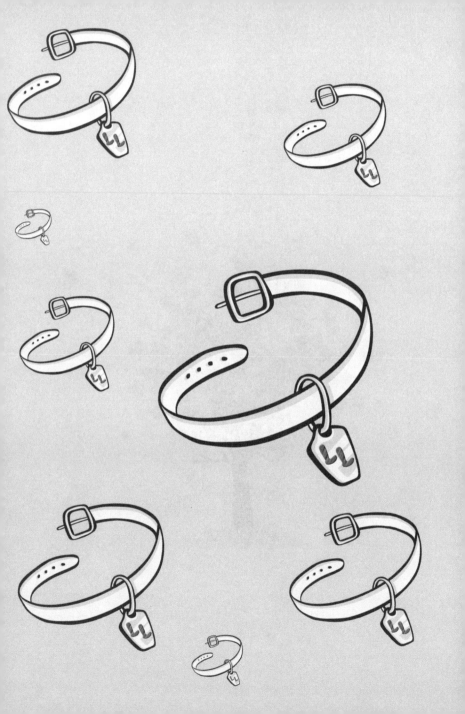

Chapter 5

DON'T GIVE UP

Lindie Lou played for a long time. She liked hiding in the colorful, crisp piles of leaves. After a while, Lindie Lou rolled on her back. She looked up at the branches above her head. They were swaying in the wind. Something else was up there. A little, brown, furry animal, with black-and-white stripes on its back, was sitting up on one of the branches. Lindie Lou watched it stuff some nuts in its cheeks. Then she watched the furry animal run to another branch. It shoved even more nuts in its cheeks. Then it darted down the tree and across the yard.

Lindie Lou looked to see where it went. She couldn't find it. Nothing moved. She waited. Still, nothing moved.

Lindie Lou rested her head on a pile of leaves and **barked**.

Suddenly, the furry little animal jumped out of the leaves and ran across the yard.

Lindie Lou chased after it. It ran up a fence. She jumped up on the fence and tried to catch it, but the chipmunk was too fast. It scurried along the fence.

Lindie Lou tried to reach it. She jumped higher and higher. She even tried to climb up on the fence, but the chipmunk was just too high.

Lindie Lou was about to give up when the chipmunk jumped off the fence and ran toward the trees. She ran after it.

Lindie Lou almost caught it when she ran over a pile of leaves and something happened.

Suddenly,

the ground felt soft underneath her feet. Before she knew it, she was falling into a hole. Lindie Lou didn't see the hole because she was watching the chipmunk.

Lindie Lou tried to climb out, but the hole was too deep. She tried to jump out, but the hole was too high. Lindie Lou sat down and looked up at the top of the hole.

What am I going to do?

She heard footsteps. Someone was walking down the sidewalk in front of Joe and Sherry's house. Lindie Lou **yowled** as loud as she could. No one answered. Then she heard the door to the Puppy Playground slam shut.

She **yowled** again.

But still, no one answered.

What if no one finds me? wondered Lindie Lou. She started to cry.

Lindie Lou tried one more time to jump out of the hole. She still couldn't jump high enough, so she dug her claws into the dirt and climbed up one side. Her eyes peeked up above the hole.

She saw Sherry in the Puppy Playground. Sherry was filling the food

and water bowls. Then she went over and played with Jasper and Diamond.

Lindie Lou was about to climb out of the hole, when her huge front paws slipped on some leaves. Lindie Lou slid down the side of the hole and landed at the bottom, again.

Lindie Lou didn't know what to do. She sat down and shook her head.

Then, Lindie Lou heard Sherry call her name. Lindie Lou

howled.

Sherry called again.

Lindie Lou **howled** even louder, but Sherry didn't hear her.

Lindie Lou tried, one more time, to climb out of the hole. She was getting very tired, but she didn't give up.

Sherry was looking out the window. She saw Lindie Lou's head pop up.

"There you are," said Sherry.

Sherry was laughing because Lindie Lou looked so funny. Her paws were full of mud and she was covered with leaves.

Lindie Lou didn't think it was funny. She wanted to get out of the hole and go back inside. She couldn't hold on anymore. She slid back in the hole. This time she rolled over and lay down. Lindie Lou was too tired to try again.

A minute later, a hand reached down into the hole, and scooped up Lindie Lou.

"I thought I filled in all the holes Molly dug," said Sherry.

She had a towel in her hand. Sherry cleaned Lindie Lou's muddy paws and pulled the leaves out of her fur.

"You're a little rascal," said Sherry. She carried Lindie Lou back into the Puppy Playground. Sherry set Lindie Lou on the floor and shook her finger at her.

"Good thing I saw you, Lindie Lou," said Sherry. "Or you would still be stuck in that hole."

Lindie Lou looked up at Sherry.

What if she hadn't seen me? thought Lindie Lou. *I think I learned another important lesson today.*

**If you try something
and fail,
keep trying.
Don't give up.**

Lindie Lou looked up at Sherry and smiled. Then she went over to the water bowl and took a drink. Jasper and Diamond walked over to Lindie Lou.

"You smell musty and muddy," said Jasper. Diamond sniffed Lindie Lou's paws.

"Time for a nap," said Sherry. She turned and walked out of the Puppy Playground. This time she closed the door tightly.

Lindie Lou was very tired. She decided to lay down on her favorite blanket. She wondered if she would ever get a chance to go outside again. She wanted to go for a ride in Joe's truck. His truck was fast . . . even faster than the chipmunk.

Lindie Lou turned and looked out the window. The tree branches were still swaying in the wind. Lindie Lou yawned, closed her eyes, and went to sleep.

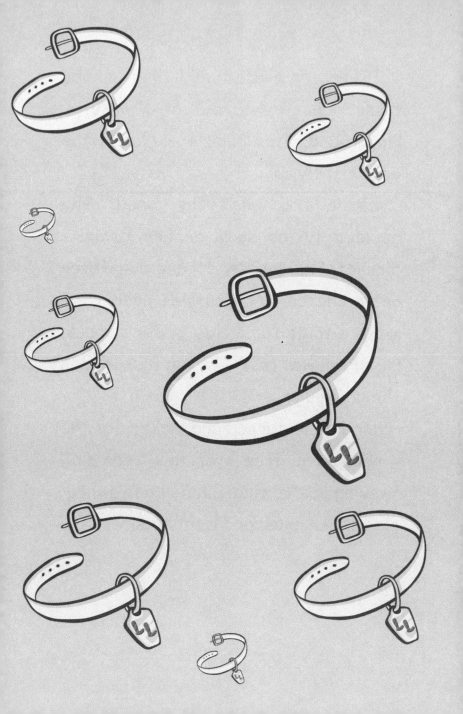

Chapter 6

A RIDE IN JOE'S TRUCK

The next morning, Lindie Lou heard a loud noise again. It sounded just like the day before. This time it didn't scare her. She knew the sound was coming from Joe's truck. She heard a door slam and some footsteps. Joe entered the Puppy Playground. He had a box in his hand. Joe picked up one of the blankets and put it in the box. Then he walked over and picked up Diamond and Jasper. Lindie Lou was sitting on the doggy bed. Joe reached over, picked her up, and put her in the box.

"Today it's your turn to go for a ride," said Joe.

Diamond and Jasper were a little afraid because they had never been outside before. Lindie Lou wondered if they were going to the same place Topaz and Ruby went the day before.

Joe carried the puppies toward his truck. He opened the door and put the box on the seat next to him.

The truck started to move. Soon, it was

moving feet.

Sometimes the ride was *smooth*. Sometimes it was **bumpy**. Lindie Lou sat up and looked out the front window. She saw houses pass by. She looked up at the sky. She saw birds

circling

in the wind. Lindie Lou curled up in the box, next to her sister Diamond, and watched the birds. She saw a cloud float by. It was shaped like a rabbit. Lindie Lou didn't know where Joe was going, but the ride in his truck was a lot of **fun**.

Jasper sat up and looked out the window. There were giant buildings in front of them.

"We're driving toward the city of Saint Louis," said Joe.

Diamond was a little afraid of the traffic noise. She sat very still in the box and looked up at Joe. He drove the truck around a corner and parked.

"We're going into that tall building," said Joe. "It's called the City Museum. You are going to meet some really nice kids today. Sherry is calling your visit, the PUPPY PLAY DATE."

Jasper looked at the City Museum. He saw a big white bird in front of the building. It was made of metal. Kids were climbing inside and waving from the windows.

Jasper looked up and saw a Ferris wheel and something strange on the corner of the building. It looked like Joe's truck except it was yellow and much bigger. It was hanging over the edge of the roof.

Joe jumped out of his truck and came around to the other side. He opened the door, picked up the box, and walked toward the building.

This looks like a crazy fun place to play, thought Lindie Lou. *I wonder if we're going to go up to the roof?*

Joe carried the puppies into the building and up the stairs. The sides of the staircase were shaped like a dinosaur. The puppies saw all kinds of cool things inside of the museum.

There was a **giant** slide, a train to ride on, and a fish the size of a car. Children were climbing in and out of the mouth of the fish. A giant slide started at the top of the building and ended on the first floor. Kids were sliding down, one at a time. They were

laughing and screaming.

"That slide is ten floors high," said Joe to the puppies.

It would be fun to play the sliding game on it, thought Jasper.

It looks too scary for me, thought Diamond.

"Look over there," said Jasper. He saw children climbing all over a bright red fire engine.

Diamond liked the art room. Kids were painting on a big piece of paper taped to the wall.

Lindie Lou saw a metal ladder with a cage around it. There were kids climbing up the ladder and disappearing into a hole in the ceiling.

In the corner was a **huge, black, rubber spider** with **wiggly** legs.

"Let's go find Sherry," said Joe. He carried the puppies down a hallway and into an office. Sherry was sitting at a desk.

"There you are," said Sherry. "You're just in time for the slide event."

"We're ready," replied Joe.

Sherry smiled and pushed a button, on the wall, near her desk.

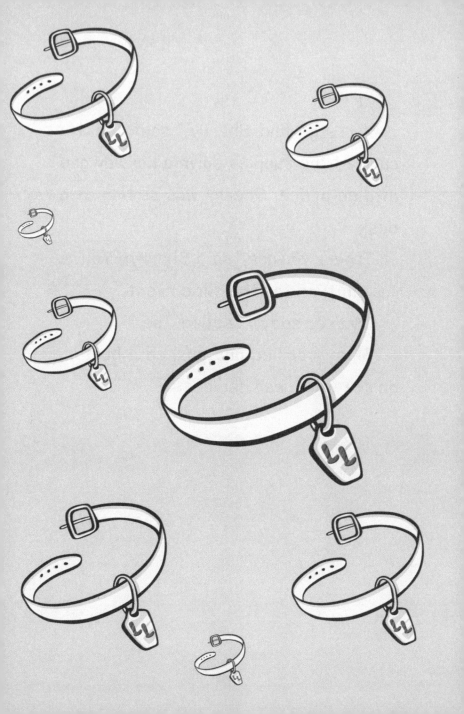

Chapter 7

AS HIGH AS THE SKY

"Good morning, everyone," announced Sherry. She was talking into a loud speaker. Her voice could be heard all over the museum. "Group leaders, please bring your children to the tenth floor for the giant slide event."

Joe, Sherry, and the puppies took the elevator to the tenth floor. Dozens of children came to greet them.

"Look at the puppies," said a little girl with curly black hair. "Can we pet them?"

"Sure, said Joe." He lowered the box so the girl could reach inside. Other children **pet** the puppies too.

Sherry and the group leaders helped the children line up.

"You're first," said Sherry.

A little boy ran to the edge of the slide.

Lindie Lou looked down at the slide. It was so curvy she couldn't see the bottom. The little boy jumped up on the slide and before anyone could say a word, he was gone.

"It's your turn," said Sherry, to the next girl in line.

"May I take one of the puppies with me?" she asked.

"I think this slide is too steep for the puppies," said Sherry. "Maybe when they're older."

"Okay," said the girl. She jumped up on the slide and disappeared around the first turn.

"Hey, wait for me," called the next boy in line. He jumped on the slide and followed the girl. The next child slid down, head first.

They continued until all the children were gone except a little girl with red hair. She looked down at the slide.

"This slide is too scary for me," she said. "May I take one of the puppies up to the rooftop?"

"Sure," said Sherry. "I'll go with you."

The little girl carefully lifted Lindie Lou out of the box.

Sherry turned to Joe.

"Could you please take the other puppies down to the first floor? We are going to meet a group of children from a local shelter. The children only stay there for a short time. They aren't allowed to have pets, so I planned a *puppy play date* for them."

"What a thoughtful idea," said Joe. "Then I'll meet you on the first floor."

Sherry smiled and nodded.

The little girl and Sherry took the

stairs up to the rooftop. Sherry pointed
to a creepy metal bug. It had six pointy
legs and **long** green wings. A little
boy was sitting on its back. The little
girl wrinkled her nose.

Sherry and the little girl walked over to a Ferris wheel.

"My name is Sherry, what's yours?"

"I'm Ava," said the little girl.

Ava sat down on one of the seats. Sherry sat next to her.

"I better hold Lindie Lou," said Sherry.

"Okay," said Ava. She handed Lindie Lou to Sherry.

A helper buckled them into their seats and pulled a bar down over their laps.

The wheel started to move.

Wow, thought Lindie Lou. We are going higher than the buildings. This must be what it feels like to fly.

The wheel went

around

and

around.

Lindie Lou liked the way it felt. Sometimes it felt like they were flying up toward the sky and other times it felt like they were falling. The wheel went around many more times. When it stopped, Ava jumped off and ran over to a big yellow school bus. It was hanging over the edge of the roof. She climbed into the driver's seat. Sherry sat next to her.

"May I hold Lindie Lou, again?" asked Ava.

"Sure," said Sherry. She set Lindie Lou on the little girl's lap.

Lindie Lou put her huge front paws on the steering wheel and looked out the window.

"We're higher than the trees," said Ava.

Oh wow, thought Lindie Lou. *We sure are high. We're as high as the sky.*

Then, a bird flew by.

We're even as high as the birds, thought Lindie Lou. *I can't wait to tell Jasper and Diamond about the cool things up here on the roof.*

Lindie Lou thought about the day before. She wondered where Joe took Topaz and Ruby. She looked around, but didn't see them. Lindie Lou wondered if she would ever see them again.

"It's time for us to go down to the cave rooms," said Sherry.

"Okay," replied Ava. "Can I carry Lindie Lou?"

"Sure," said Sherry, "but be very careful with her."

Ava followed Sherry over to the elevator. The inside was painted like a

They entered the elevator and Sherry pushed a button.

"First floor, here we come," said Ava.

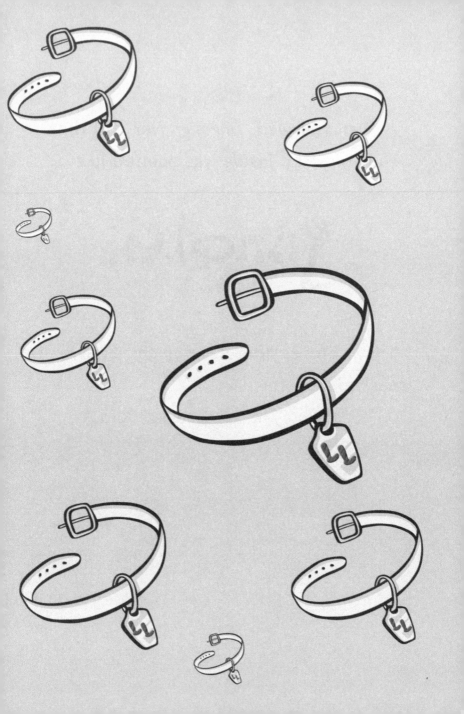

Chapter 8

THE PUPPY PLAY DATE

When the elevator doors opened, Sherry, Lindie Lou, and Ava were on the first floor. There were fish, turtles, and a whale painted on the wall. The ceiling was full of pointy mirror pieces. They were hanging down and looked like shiny stones. The floor was covered with many colorful tiles. Some looked like fish,

some looked like waves.

There were huge fish to climb on and tunnels to crawl through. One tunnel led to a room with a beautiful mermaid fountain in the middle. An underground river flowed into all of the rooms. The sound of SPLASHING WATER and children playing could be heard everywhere.

Sherry led Ava through an opening and into another room. Joe was waiting for them. He was holding the box with Diamond and Jasper in it. Ava put Lindie Lou in the box.

"Follow me," said Joe. "The children are waiting for us in the next room. They are very excited to meet the puppies."

"Okay," said Sherry. "Then they're ready for our *puppy play date.*"

Joe nodded. He carried the puppies through a hole in one of the walls. He had to bend down because the entrance was so small. On the other side was another cave room. An orange spotlight lit the room.

A dozen children and a few teenage helpers, were sitting in a circle. Joe walked into the circle. He set the box, with the puppies in it, on the floor. Then Joe walked over to the side of the room near Sherry.

"It's storytelling time with the puppies," said Sherry. "Who would like to go first?"

A little boy raised his hand. Sherry nodded. The boy stood up, walked over to the box of puppies, and picked up Jasper.

"Once upon a time, there was a puppy named..."

"Jasper," said Sherry.

"Jasper," replied the little boy.

"Jasper was a playful puppy. He also liked to fly!"

The little boy held Jasper up in the air and acted like he was flying.

All the children

laughed and clapped.

"Who's next?" asked Sherry.

"May I have a turn?" asked a girl in a blue shirt.

"Yes," said Sherry.

The little girl picked up Diamond.

"Once upon a time there was a puppy named..."

"Diamond," said Joe.

"Diamond," replied the little girl.

She looked at Diamond, who was rolled up like a ball.

"Diamond is very shy, just like me."

The girl sat down. She rested Diamond on her lap. Diamond looked up at the little girl and smiled.

"Aww," replied the children.

Sherry nodded at Ava. She walked into the middle of the circle and picked up Lindie Lou.

"This puppy's name is Lindie Lou," said Ava. "Sherry and I took her up to the roof. We rode on the Ferris wheel together. Then we sat in the school bus."

"Nice," said one of the children.

"Look at her **big** paws," said Ava. "Lindie Lou steered the school bus with these." Ava held up one of Lindie Lou's paws.

"Cool," replied a boy in a green shirt.

Sherry walked into the center of the circle near Ava.

"If you are very careful, we'll pass the puppies around," said Sherry.

"Yay," clapped the children.

"Would you like to learn a song?" asked Sherry.

"Sure," replied the children.

"Okay," said Sherry. "When I finish the verses, you can sing...

♪ ♪ L-I-N-D-I-E L-O-U ♪ ♪
spells Lindie Lou."

"Okay," replied the children. They clapped their hands.

When they were finished singing, Sherry turned the lights up. She picked up some books and handed them to the children. They took turns reading to each other.

Joe and Sherry smiled as they walked around the cave room. The children held the puppies, one at a time. Jasper rolled over on a little boy's lap. He rubbed Jasper's tummy. Diamond jumped back into the box. She peeked out over the top and looked at all the children. Lindie Lou wagged her tail so fast, it made the children giggle.

After a nice long visit, Joe picked up the puppies and put them back in the box. The group leaders lined up the children to say goodbye. They pet the puppies one last time. Joe and Sherry waved to the children. Then they left the room.

Later, on the way home, Joe and Sherry talked about their day.

"The children really enjoyed the *puppy play date*," said Joe.

"They sure did," said Sherry. "Thank you for bringing them."

"You're welcome," replied Joe. He smiled and winked at her.

Sherry turned and looked at the puppies.

Jasper, Diamond, and Lindie Lou were sound *asleep* in the box, in the back seat of Joe's truck.

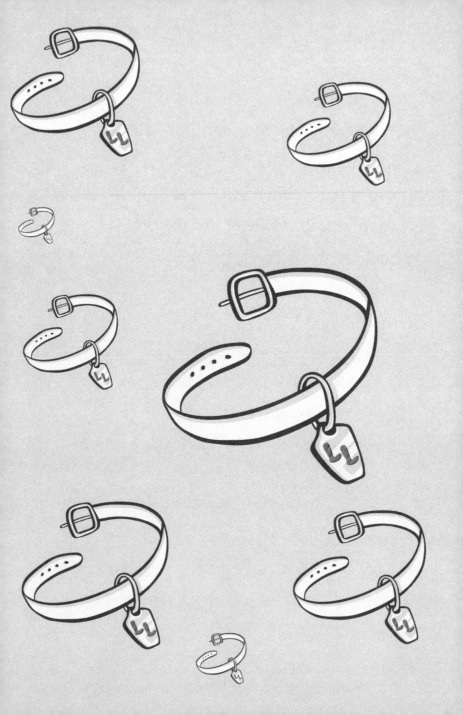

Chapter 9

WHERE AM I GOING?

The next morning, Lindie Lou heard someone walking toward the Puppy Playground. The door opened and Joe came in. He went over to Lindie Lou and folded his arms.

"It's your turn to leave," said Joe.

Lindie Lou ran over to Coco, picked him up in her mouth, and sat at Joe's feet.

Maybe we're going to meet up with Topaz and Ruby, thought Lindie Lou. She looked at Joe with curious eyes.

Joe reached down and picked up Lindie Lou. He grabbed Coco out of her mouth and tossed him into the box of stuffed animals.

Lindie Lou wasn't going to leave without Coco! She twisted out of Joe's hands and jumped to the floor. Then she ran to the box of stuffed animals. Lindie Lou grabbed Coco and walked back to Joe. She sat down at his feet. Lindie Lou looked up at Joe as if to say...

If I go, he goes.

Joe put his hands on his hips and nodded.

"Okay girl, if that stuffed monkey means so much to you, it can come too."

Joe picked them up and headed for the door.

Lindie Lou turned around and looked at Jasper and Diamond. She barked goodbye.

Diamond and Jasper were sitting on the doggy bed.

Diamond barked back.

Jasper rolled over and looked at Lindie Lou.

Lindie Lou wanted to play with Jasper, but Joe was walking toward the door. He left the Puppy Playground with Lindie Lou and Coco under his arm.

Joe closed the door and walked over to his truck. He put Lindie Lou and Coco in the same cardboard box she was in the day before. The box was on the seat next to Joe.

"Wait a minute," called Sherry. She ran over to the truck. "Here are some things to remember us by."

Sherry opened the door and lifted Lindie Lou and Coco out of the box. She spread a blanket on the bottom of the box and set Lindie Lou and Coco on top.  Lindie Lou sniffed the blanket. It was her favorite.

Then Sherry took a collar out of her pocket. She put it around Lindie Lou's

neck. A metal tag hung from the collar. The letters "LL" were printed on the tag. Lindie Lou wiggled her head and the tag jingled. Sherry giggled. Then she leaned down and rubbed noses with Lindie Lou.

Sherry closed the door and backed away from the truck.

Lindie Lou put her huge paws on the

edge of the cardboard box. She stood up so she could look out of the window. She saw Molly sitting by Sherry.

Sherry wiped a tear from her cheek. Jasper and Diamond were playing the sliding game in the Puppy Playground.

Lindie Lou pushed away from the window and lay down next to Coco. She wanted to go for a ride, but she wanted to stay too.

Where am I going? she wondered. *Will I ever see my family again?*

The truck drove away from the orange brick house with the green front lawn and the colorful trees.

Lindie Lou looked up at Joe. He took a treat out of his pocket, and gave it to Lindie Lou.

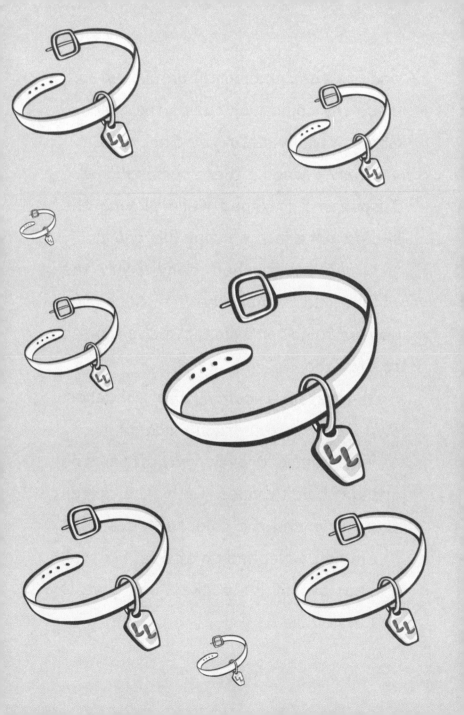

Chapter 10

TAP, TAP, TAP

The truck was moving fast. Faster than the day before.

Lindie Lou looked up at the sky. There were clouds everywhere.

I wonder what it's like to be as high as the clouds, thought Lindie Lou. *When we were at the City Museum, we were as high as the sky, and as high as the birds. But the clouds were even higher.*

Lindie Lou looked down at Coco.

I wish I knew where we were going, she thought. She felt the truck slow down. Joe made a wide turn and then stopped. Lindie Lou watched Joe jump out of the truck. He opened the back door and picked up a pink box.

"This carrier is for you, Lindie Lou," he said.

Joe opened Lindie Lou's door, lifted her out of the cardboard box, and put her blanket and Coco in the pink carrier. Then Joe carefully placed Lindie Lou inside the

carrier and closed the door.

Lindie Lou sniffed around. The inside smelled like a plastic toy she played with in the Puppy Playground. There were many holes in the sides for her to look out of. Each hole was about the size of a strawberry. The door was made of metal. It had crisscross wire covering it. Lindie Lou stuck her nose out one of the holes and took a sniff. She smelled fresh air.

Joe picked up her carrier and walked toward a gray-and-white building.

"You are going to live in the Emerald City with Sherry's sister Kate and her husband Bryan," said Joe.

Suddenly, a low-flying airplane flew above their heads.

"There goes an airplane," said Joe.

It looks like the big white bird we saw at the city museum, thought Lindie Lou.

The noise was so...

LOUD

Lindie Lou had to cover her ears with her huge front paws.

"An airplane is going to take you to the Emerald City," said Joe. He pointed up into the sky.

Lindie Lou looked up through the door of her carrier. She saw another airplane...

They sure are loud, thought Lindie Lou.

Joe carried Lindie Lou into the gray-and-white building. He walked over to a long silver counter. The lady behind the counter had **SUSIE** printed on her name tag. Lindie Lou heard Joe say, "Good morning."

"Good morning. Welcome to the Saint Louis Airport," said Susie. She leaned over and looked inside the carrier. Lindie Lou saw Susie smiling at her.

Joe looked through the door of the carrier.

"Susie will take good care of you."

"Yes, I will," said Susie. "You are

going to have fun today because you're going on an amazing ride."

Lindie Lou heard Susie tape something to the top of her carrier.

"You're going to have a good life", said Joe. "Wait until you see the Emerald City. It's a wonderful place to live."

Joe put his finger through one of the holes in her carrier.

Lindie Lou licked his finger.

Susie handed some papers to Joe.

"Okay girl, you're ready to go," said Joe. He tapped on the top of the carrier. Tap, tap, tap, was his way of saying,

I love you!

Lindie Lou watched Joe walk away.

Just before Joe left the airport, he looked over his shoulder and winked at Lindie Lou.

Lindie Lou watched Joe leave the building. She started to cry.

"Don't worry Lindie Lou. You're going to be okay," said Susie. She put her finger through the door of the carrier and pet Lindie Lou's nose. "Wait till you see your new home. You are going to love it. There are many green trees and lots of green parks for you to play in. It's why they call it the Emerald City."

Emerald City

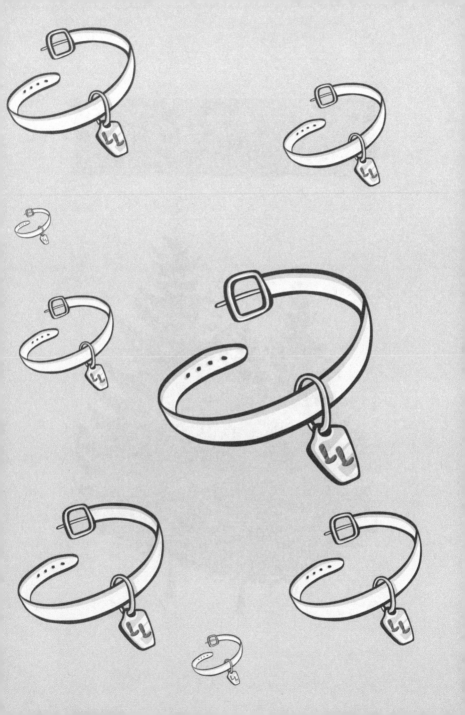

Chapter 11

THE BIG WHITE BIRD

Lindie Lou looked around the airport. Everything was white. The lights were white. The pictures on the walls were white. The floors were white. Even the ceiling was white. The only colors Lindie Lou saw were on the people walking by. Lindie Lou looked across the room. She saw a giant window.

Oh, there are all the colors, she thought.

Outside of the window was a long row of pots. Bright red, yellow, and purple flowers grew out of the pots. Colorful trees lined the road. Suddenly Lindie Lou wanted to go outside. She

scratched

on her carrier. She **ran in circles.**

She tried to find a way out.

"It's okay, little one," said Susie. Her kind voice calmed Lindie Lou. She sat down on her blanket near Coco and took a deep breath.

After a while, Susie picked up the carrier and placed it on a conveyor belt.

Lindie Lou was on the move. She went around a corner, through a sliding door, and down a long tunnel. At the end of the tunnel was another sliding door. She traveled through this door too. Then her carrier stopped.

Lindie Lou wondered where she was. It was dark and very quiet. She looked out of one of the holes in her carrier, but Lindie Lou couldn't see anything.

She was scared!

Lindie Lou listened and waited for someone to come. But no one did. Lindie Lou wondered if she would ever go outside again. She thought about her brothers and sisters and the Puppy Playground. Lindie Lou missed them and wanted to go back.

Lindie Lou waited and waited. No one came. She put her head down and whimpered softly. Then she curled up next to Coco.

I'm glad Coco is here, thought Lindie Lou. *What if I have to spend the rest of my life in this dark place?*

Lindie Lou closed her eyes and sighed.

More time passed.

Finally, Lindie Lou heard a loud rumbling noise. It sounded like Joe's truck. *Was he coming to get her?*

A door swung open and light filled the room.

Lindie Lou saw a man driving a noisy tractor. It was pulling a cart.

The tractor stopped a few feet away from Lindie Lou's carrier.

Then, a *dog* barked!

Is there another dog in here? wondered Lindie Lou. She tried to look around.

The man jumped off of the tractor. He walked over to Lindie Lou and picked up her carrier. Then he opened the back of the cart and slid Lindie Lou inside. There was another pet carrier in the cart. Lindie Lou saw the face of another dog.

The man closed the door in the back of the cart and walked out of the building. He closed the door behind him.

"Hello, I'm Lindie Lou," barked Lindie Lou softly.

"Hi, I'm Max," answered the dog.

"This place is dark, and I'm scared," said Lindie Lou.

"Don't be afraid. This is only a small part of the airport, the darkest part. Most of it is bright and friendly."

"When will it be light again?" asked Lindie Lou.

"When the man comes back and drives us outside."

"Oh," replied Lindie Lou. "Have you been here before?"

"Yes," answered Max. "When we get outside, you will see the most amazing thing."

"I will?" asked Lindie Lou. "What's out there?"

"Some people call them big white birds," said Max. "They can fly and they're enormous! Actually, they're airplanes."

"Airplanes?" asked Lindie Lou. "I saw some of them flying over us on the way to the airport."

"Have you ever been inside one?" asked Max.

"No," replied Lindie Lou, "but I saw some children playing inside an airplane at the City Museum."

"Was it moving?" asked Max.

"No," said Lindie Lou.

"Well these birds can move," howled Max. "They move so fast they can fly. And we're going to ride inside an airplane today."

"We are? I knew we could go inside an airplane, but I didn't know they could fly with us inside," said Lindie Lou.

"They sure can," replied Max. "One of these big white birds will take us thousands of miles away from here. In less than a day."

Lindie Lou gasped.

"Wow, we're actually going to travel up into the sky?"

"Yes," said Max.

"We're going to fly?" asked Lindie Lou.

"Not us," replied Max. "The airplane is and you're going to love the ride."

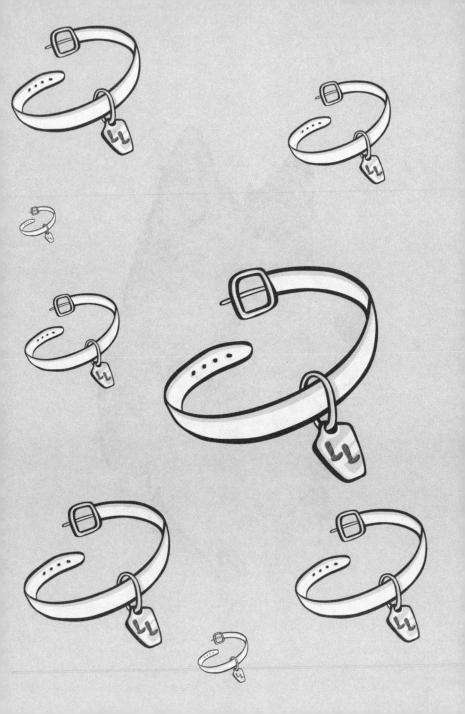

Chapter 12

FLYING HIGH

A door opened and the man who drove the tractor came back into the room. Lindie Lou and Max were quietly waiting. He climbed onto the tractor and started the engine. The man drove up to a large door. The door rolled up and light filled the room.

The light was so bright, Lindie Lou couldn't see. She put her head down and covered her eyes. Then, very slowly she moved her paws away from her face.

There it was....right in front of her.

A BIG WHITE BIRD

It was bright and shiny.

The man drove the tractor out of the building. He drove to the bottom of a ramp, near the big white bird. The man stopped the tractor and jumped down to the ground. He walked around to the back of the cart, picked up Lindie Lou's carrier, and placed it on the moving ramp.

Lindie Lou was going up into the belly of the airplane. Another man

was waiting inside. He grabbed Lindie Lou's carrier, placed it on a bench, and strapped it down. Her carrier was right next to a window.

Then Max's carrier came up the ramp. He was strapped right next to Lindie Lou.

Max was sitting up so tall, his ears touched the top of his carrier.

Lindie Lou could see his light-blue eyes through the holes in his carrier. She thought he was quite handsome. She also thought he looked very wise.

"I'm eight weeks old," said Lindie Lou. "May I ask how old you are?"

"I'm eleven years old, which is quite old in dog years," said Max.

Max was looking around. He was watching everything. Boxes were being brought in and piled up all around them. Each one was strapped down tight. Then the man left the airplane, shut the door, and locked it.

Lindie Lou turned to Max.

"You said we are going to a

faraway place?"

"Yes," replied Max. "Very far away."

Lindie Lou remembered Susie telling her she was going to her new home in

Emerald City. This must be how she was going to get there.

Lindie Lou looked around the airplane.

"I'm a little afraid," said Lindie Lou.

"You don't have to be," replied Max. "Airplanes are amazing. They take people, animals, and things all over the world. I've been on many amazing journeys and you will too. This is only the beginning."

Then Lindie Lou heard the engines start up.

"Airplanes are noisy," barked Lindie Lou.

"It takes a lot of power to fly a big bird like this," replied Max.

Lindie Lou felt the plane move. It went faster and faster. It went so fast, it lifted up into the sky.

"We're flying," said Max.

"Flying high," cheered Lindie Lou.

YOU ARE A

VERY LUCKY GIRL

CUZ YOU'RE GOING

ALL OVER THE WORLD

La La La

La La La La La

La La La

La La

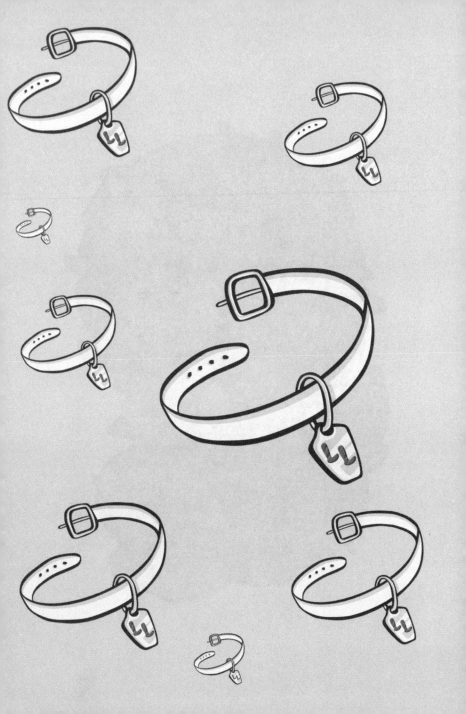

Chapter 13

WHAT A VIEW

SAINT LOUIS, MISSOURI

The big white bird flew up into the clear blue sky. It flew over the city of Saint Louis.

"Oh, wow," said Lindie Lou. "The view is amazing from up here."

The plane turned to the right.

"Whoa, are we falling?" asked Lindie Lou.

"No, we're turning," replied Max.

Then the plane straightened out.

Lindie Lou pushed Coco into a corner.

He'll be safer there, thought Lindie Lou.

The noise from the airplane was loud but steady. Lindie Lou looked over at Max. He was moving with the plane.

Lindie Lou thought she would be afraid, but she was beginning to enjoy the ride.

"We're on our way to the Emerald City," barked Max.

"Where is it?" asked Lindie Lou. She was looking out of the window.

"Relax," replied Max. "We will have to fly for a few more hours before you'll be able to see it."

"Look," said Lindie Lou.

She saw a giant metal object curving up into the sky.

"It's the Gateway Arch," said Max. "You can take a ride to the top in an elevator shaped like an egg."

I'd like to go for a ride in that elevator, thought Lindie Lou. She looked down and tried to see everything. Then the plane took a gentle right turn.

A little farther on, Lindie Lou saw a large green area.

"That's Forest Park," said Max. "It's

one of the largest city parks in the United States."

"It's huge," yipped Lindie Lou.

"There are many trails and lots of places to run and play in that beautiful park," said Max.

"Look to the left," said Max. "It's the Saint Louis Zoo."

"What's a zoo?" asked Lindie Lou.

"A zoo is a place where wild animals live. The word *zoo* came from the Greek word *zoon*, which means animal. People like to go there to see the animals up close."

"I can see many animals," replied Lindie Lou.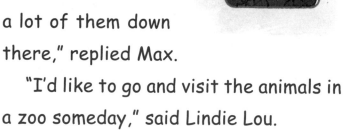

"There sure are a lot of them down there," replied Max.

"I'd like to go and visit the animals in a zoo someday," said Lindie Lou.

"Can you see the elephants, giraffes, and rhinos?" asked Max. "They're the ones over by the water hole."

"Yes," replied Lindie Lou. "They look like toys from way up here."

The airplane flew over a large pink area.

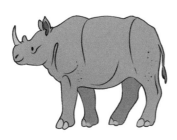

"Wow! What's over there?" asked Lindie Lou.

"A flock of birds called flamingos," said Max. "They stand on one leg when they sleep."

"They're pink because they eat a lot of shellfish called shrimp."

"Maybe if I ate shrimp, I'd turn pink," barked Lindie Lou.

"You look just fine the way you are," replied Max.

"I would like to chase the flamingos!" howled Lindie Lou. She jumped up and

her head on the top of her carrier.

"You will have a lot of chances to chase birds at your new home," said Max.

"I will?" asked Lindie Lou.

"Yes," replied Max. "Are you enjoying the ride?"

"Very much," answered Lindie Lou.

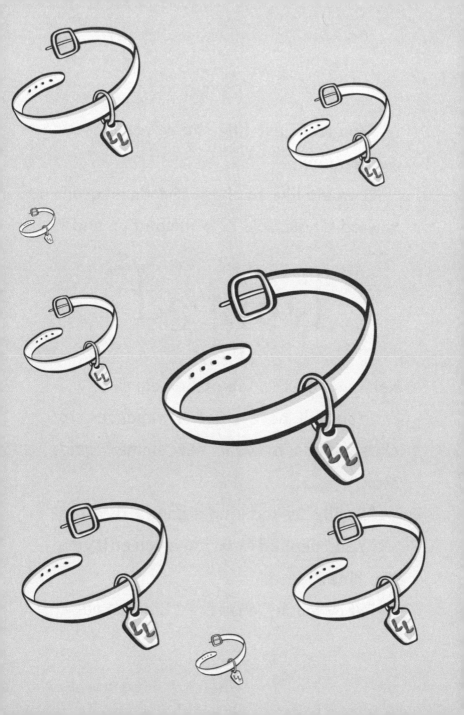

Chapter 14

ALMOST THERE

The front of the airplane tipped up and flew higher. Lindie Lou watched objects on the ground become smaller and smaller.

The airplane flew above the clouds. Then, the engines slowed down and the sound coming from the airplane was much softer. Lindie Lou watched....

 clouds float by.

So this is what it's like to be as high as the clouds, thought Lindie Lou.

The sun was shining above the clouds and the sky was blue. A beam of light lit up the inside of the airplane.

"It's so peaceful up here," said Lindie Lou.

"Now you know why I like to fly," replied Max.

Lindie Lou moved with the motion of the plane, just like Max. She WAS enjoying the ride.

Time passed. The airplane flew smoothly above the clouds. Lindie Lou looked ahead of the plane.

"Are we almost there?"

"Not yet," replied Max. "I'll let you know when we get close."

"What's the Emerald City like?" asked Lindie Lou.

"Hmm," said Max. "Let me give you a few hints. It's a very big city in the state of Washington. It's next to a giant volcano and there's a famous landmark called Pike Place Market."

"Do you live there?" asked Lindie Lou.

"Yes, I live downtown near the market."

"Do you like living there?"

"Yes, very much."

"Why were you in Saint Louis?"

"My owner's father lives there. We went for a visit. My owner is flying on another airplane. They didn't have room for my carrier. That's why I'm flying on this plane."

"What's it like living near the market?"

"It's great," said Max. "I get free smoked fish from a man named Harry."

"You eat fish?"

"Yes. The smoked flavor is very tasty and I like the bones in it. You'll have to try it sometime."

"Okay," replied Lindie Lou.

"There's a girl who works in the market named Delight. She gives me left-over bones from her restaurant."

"Her name is Delight?"

"Yes, she is very sweet. Some of her friends call her Delightful."

"Woo hoo!" howled Lindie Lou. "I would like to eat at the market and meet your friends."

"Maybe some day, when you're a little older," said Max.

"Right now you should try to sleep. When we get closer, I'll wake you up."

"Okay," replied Lindie Lou. She put her head on Coco and closed her eyes.

"What will happen when we get there?"

"An airport helper will take us into a room where our owners will come to meet us. Then, they'll drive us home."

"Home," sighed Lindie Lou. She liked the way the word sounded. She looked over at Max. "I'm glad you're here," said Lindie Lou. "This ride would have been scary without you."

"I'm happy I could help you enjoy your first flight," said Max.

Lindie Lou took a deep breath. Just before she fell asleep, she heard Max say...

"I can promise you this. Your life has only just begun little one."

I CAN'T WAIT
TO SEE
WHERE YOU
TAKE ME
La La La
La La La La La
La La La
La La

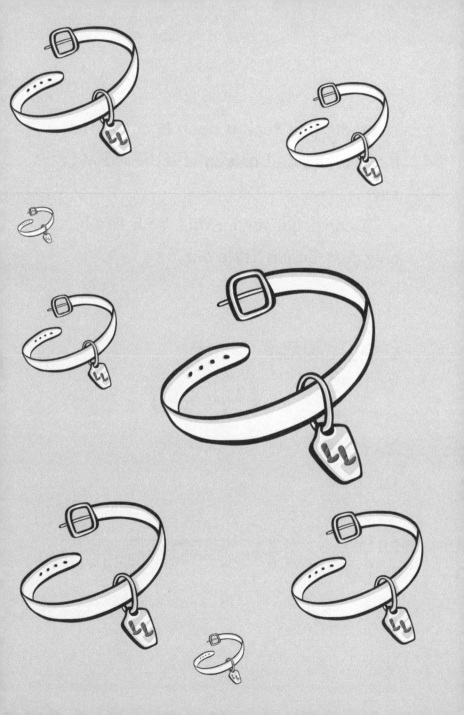

Chapter 15

A VOLCANO

"Time to wake up," barked Max.

Lindie Lou shook her head and looked around. She was dreaming about the Puppy Playground. She almost forgot she was on an airplane.

"There it is," yelled Max.

Lindie Lou looked out the window. A giant mountain stood in the distance.

"It's a volcano and it's called Mount Rainier."

"What's all the white stuff on top of it?" asked Lindie Lou.

"Snow," barked Max. "Tiny pieces of frozen water is called snow. When the snow melts, it turns into water. Do you see how high it is?"

"Yes," answered Lindie Lou. "The volcano is almost as high as we are."

"Most volcanos have flat tops," said Max.

"Why?" asked Lindie Lou.

"Because, down near the center of the earth, rocks heat up. When they get hot enough, they shoot up from under the ground and out of the top of volcanoes. These hot rocks blow the tops off of volcanos."

"Why would they do that?" asked Lindie Lou.

"To release pressure," replied Max. "Did you know that the entire earth was formed this way?"

"From hot rocks shooting out of the top of volcanoes?"

"Exactly," barked Max.

"Are we going to see it blow up?"

"Not today," replied Max. "Most volcanoes let off steam before they blow up."

"Good," replied Lindie Lou. She watched the volcano as they slowly passed by.

"Get ready for our landing."

What's a landing? wondered Lindie Lou.

The front of the airplane tipped down. Lindie Lou held her breath.

After a few seconds she asked, "Are we falling?"

"We're landing," said Max.

THUD was the sound the plane made when it landed. Lindie Lou jumped to her feet. **Swoosh** was the sound the airplane made as it slowed down. Lindie Lou slid to the back of her carrier near Coco. Then the plane rolled along the runway.

"I'm glad I didn't know about this part," said Lindie Lou.

"I think it's the coolest part!" barked Max.

The plane slowed down. It passed a few buildings, turned left, and stopped.

"We have arrived in the Emerald City," said Max.

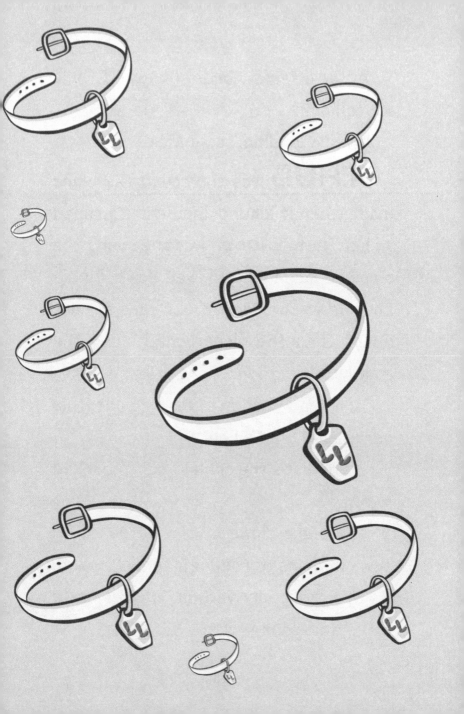

Chapter 16

LANDED

"Why has the airplane stopped?" asked Lindie Lou.

"Because our flight is finished. Someone will come very soon and unload us," replied Max.

Lindie Lou sat very still and waited.

Wow, I've sure learned a lot of life lessons lately, thought Lindie Lou.

The most important one was...

To overcome your fears,
stop, look around, and listen.
Think about what you can do.
Do something if you need to.
If nothing can be done,
stay calm and think
of something good.

*　　*　　*　　*　　*

"Lindie Lou must have landed by now,"
said Joe to Sherry.

"Kate called," replied Sherry. "She's on her way to the airport."

"Good," replied Joe.

"Diamond should be landing in about an hour," said Sherry.

"Yes, I checked her flight. It's on time," replied Joe. "Rod and Roma are the perfect owners for Diamond. Roma's a bit shy and so is Diamond. They are an ideal match."

"And they both have black hair," giggled Sherry. A tear ran down her cheek.

"I already miss the puppies," said Joe.

"So do I," said Sherry. She put her head on Joe's shoulder. "Can we go and visit them soon?"

"Sure," replied Joe. He put his arm around her.

Sherry looked over at the Puppy Playground.

"I'm glad we kept Jasper. He's the only puppy we have left. It won't be the same for him without his brothers and sisters."

"I checked on Jasper before we sat down," replied Joe. "He was fine. Molly was with him."

"Oh good," replied Sherry.

The sun set behind the trees and the sky slowly turned a deep blue color. Joe and Sherry watched the stars *twinkle* above their heads.

"It's time to go inside," said Joe. He stood up and reached for Sherry's hand.

"Let's stop and say goodnight to Molly and Jasper," said Sherry.

"Great idea," replied Joe.

They walked together, hand in hand toward the Puppy Playground.

QUICK QUIZ

1. In what city was Lindie Lou born?

2. Where does Lindie Lou play with her brothers and sisters?

3. What is the name of Lindie Lou's pet monkey?

4. Which of the puppies is the shy one?

5. Why didn't Joe and Sherry keep Lindie Lou?

6. What did Lindie Lou take to her new home to make her feel more loved?

7. Why did the author create the character, Max?

8. How do Lindie Lou's huge paws help her?

9. After reading the hints in the book, where do you think Lindie Lou's new home is?

10. Which puppy did Joe and Sherry keep?

Answers:

(1) Saint Louis (2) The Puppy Playground (3) Coco (4) Diamond (5) Promised her to Sherry's sister Kate (6) Coco, favorite blanket (7) To take away Lindie Lou's fear (8) Show off, rest her head, win the game, hang on, cover her eyes, climb (9) Seattle, Washington (10) Jasper.

Fun Facts

Saint Louis, Missouri

- Ice-cream cones, hot dogs, and iced tea were first introduced at the 1904 Saint Louis World's Fair.

- The first Olympic Games in the United States were held in Saint Louis in 1904.

- The state of Missouri is known as the Cave State. There are over one hundred reported caves in Saint Louis County.

- Take the tram ride to the top of the Gateway Arch, the tallest national monument in the United States at 630 feet.

- Things to do in Forest Park:
  - The Saint Louis Zoo
  - Saint Louis Science Center
  - Art & History Museums
  - The Jewel Box, a plant and flower greenhouse.
  - The Trolley is a great way to move around the park.

Saint Louis • Calendar

January
THE LOOP ICE CARNIVAL.
A celebration with ice carving
demonstrations, scavenger
hunts, s'mores roast, human
dogsled races, and ice slides for
the kids. www.visittheloop.com

March
ANNUAL SAINT PATRICK'S
DAY PARADE AND RUN. Five-
mile parade with huge balloons,
floats, and a marching band.
www.irishparade.org

February
MAPLE SUGAR FESTIVAL.
Sponsored by the Missouri
Department of Conservation.
Kids can learn how to make
maple syrup by tapping into
maple trees and boiling the
sap into syrup. Try the "sugar
on snow," warm maple syrup
drizzled on a snowball. http://
saintlouis.kidsoutandabout.com/
content/maple-sugar-festival-1

SOULARD MARDI GRAS.
A celebration full of masks,
dancing, parades, sports
competitions, and more!
www.mardigrasinc.com

April
GO! SAINT LOUIS MARATHON
& FAMILY FITNESS WEEKEND.
Weekend full of fun and fitness
for all ages and abilities.
www.gostlouis.org

SAINT LOUIS EARTH DAY
FESTIVAL. Celebration
with more than two hundred
booths and activities all
aimed at educating people on
environmental issues. www.
stlouisearthday.org

May

ART FAIR AT LAUMEIER.
Nationally acclaimed arts and crafts fair. It represents various art forms and includes a kids' area, a Creation Station, demonstrations, and live music and entertainment. www.laumeier.com

June

CIRCUS FLORA. A truly American one-ring circus with sawdust floors and big top tent. Named after one lucky elephant named Flora. www.circusflora.org

July

FAIR SAINT LOUIS. Fourth of July celebration. America's biggest birthday party draws twenty-five thousand visitors with free concerts, vendors, and an elaborate fireworks display. www.fairsaintlouis.org

August

FESTIVAL OF NATIONS.
Celebration featuring forty ethnic food booths, music, arts and crafts, and an international bazaar. www.festivalofnationsstl.org

September

LOUFEST MUSIC FESTIVAL.
A sustainability festival for all ages. Area K is a special area designated for kids, featuring food, rock climbing, magic, and music. www.loufest.com

October

STUCKMEYER'S FARM.
Annual event in the fall that includes a pumpkin patch, a barrel-train ride, pony rides, farm animals, hayrides, and live music. www.stuckmeyers.com/index.htm

November

WAY OF LIGHTS. A mile-and-a-half scenic drive showcasing over a million holiday lights, a petting zoo, a laser light show, and a display of Christmas trees full of lights and decorations. www.wayoflights.org

December

FIRST NIGHT SAINT LOUIS.
New Year's Eve celebration for the whole family, with performing arts, magicians, storytellers, musicians, puppeteers, and fireworks. www.grandcenter.org/first-night-program

Places to go with:

Pets

-and-

Pet-Friendly

Hotels in...

Saint Louis, Missouri

Find links to dog parks, pet-friendly hotels, restaurants, and dog sitters on our website:

http://lindielou.com/places-to-go.html

Lindie Lou®
Adventure Series

- ## Book 1: FLYING HIGH
  Flying on an Airplane for the Very First Time!

  Lindie Lou is a curious puppy who dreams of seeing the world. She lives in a "Puppy Playground" with her brothers and sisters. One day, Lindie Lou learns she is being adopted by a family who lives far-away. Soon she is "Flying High" on an airplane for the very first time!

- ## Book 2: UP IN SPACE
  An Adventure at the Space Needle!

  Follow Lindie Lou through the city of Seattle, where she meets-up with an old friend, meets new friends and learns life lessons along the way. Join in the fun when Lindie Lou discovers Rachel the Pig, sees flying fish, orca whales and the gum wall. But her biggest adventure awaits... when she goes UP IN SPACE.

- ## Book 3: HARVEST TIME
  A Celebration on an Organic Farm!

  Lindie Lou has no idea what an organic farm is like. While visiting Cousin Ronda, she discovers a whole new way of living. Join in the fun! Lindie Lou enjoys the thrill of a hayloft, the challenge of a corn maze, the celebration of the harvest, and the dangers of a combine. Her family and friends play together, solve problems together, even save each other's lives!

- ## Book 4 : BIG CITY MAGIC
  Uncover the Secret of the Big Apple!

  Guess where Lindie Lou finds the big apple? Hint...it's in a city called "The Big Apple." Send your guesses to... www.lindielou.com/blog.html

About the Author and the Illustrator

JEANNE BENDER
Author

Jeanne Bender loves to travel. While exploring the world, she experienced many incredible things. Bender decided to write about her adventures through the eyes of her puppy Lindie Lou.

Lindie Lou traveled with author Jeanne Bender to many places around the world. Their experiences became the inspiration of the *Lindie Lou Adventure Series.*

Bender's education began early on when she received high praise for her poetry and early composition. Later she studied with a creative writing professor in Seattle, Washington, and continued her education in the United Kingdom at Oxford University.

Bender's beginning chapter books titled the *Lindie Lou Adventure Series,* were first introduced to elementary school students grades K-5.

Bender first experienced *"**Lindie Lou Mania"*** when students told her they loved her stories and the characters and wanted to read more about them. Everywhere Bender went she was humbled when children lined up to buy her books.

KATE WILLOWS
Illustrator

Kate Willows loves drawing and coloring things on her computer. She creates animals and cartoons for everyone to enjoy, including all the Lindie Lou characters.

Willows graduated from The Ohio State University with a degree in art technology and a minor in design. Kate also works for a gaming company and does amazing drawings.

She enjoys playing video games and reading in her spare time. Kate lives near Columbus, Ohio, with her two cats Nyx and Nico.